Barbro Lindgren

SHORTY TAKES OFF

Illustrated by Olof Landström

Translated by Richard E. Fisher

R&S
BOOKS

Stockholm   New York   London   Adelaide   Toronto

Rabén & Sjögren Stockholm

Translation copyright © 1990 by Richard E. Fisher
All rights reserved
Illustrations copyright © 1989 by Olof Landström
Originally published in Sweden by Rabén & Sjögren under the title *Sunkan flyger,*
text copyright © 1989 by Barbro Lindgren
Library of Congress catalog card number: 90-60423
Printed in Singapore
First edition, 1990

ISBN 91 29 59770 6

R & S Books are distributed in the United States of America
by Farrar, Straus and Giroux, New York;
in the United Kingdom by Ragged Bears, Andover;
in Canada by Vanwell Publishing, St. Catharines
and in Australia by ERA Publications, Adelaide

Everything had gone wrong for Shorty.

The cat had run away. His mom had been mean to him. His dad had gone to the junkyard to get rid of the Volvo van Shorty was supposed to get when he grew up. A dog had run off with his soccer ball.

There was no more Coca-Cola. The french fries were all gone.

He had nothing left but a couple of sticks to poke into holes and a few tin cans to rattle.

While he poked his sticks into holes and rattled his cans, he thought how unfair it was that he should have a mean mom and a dumb dad and no soccer ball and a cat which had run away.

And he wished that at least he was a little taller, so he wouldn't get lost whenever he walked around the block.

But still, that's the way it was. He was no taller than a stick, and as soon as he went out of the house, he got lost and had to cry rivers of tears until someone found him.

If only he had wings. Then there'd be no problem. Then he would soar out over the roofs effortlessly without getting lost. He would fly over the junkyard and look for the Volvo van. And over the woods, where his cat was probably sitting in a tree, crying.

How did the birds do it? How did they manage to have wings when they were still in the egg? Why didn't he have any, when he wanted them so badly?

While he walked around and looked for his cat and his soccer ball and poked his sticks into holes and rattled his cans, he kept thinking about his wings. How could he get them to grow? That was the big question.

One night, when his dad was at an office party and his mom was on the phone, talking with an old school friend, Shorty lay in bed thinking about those wings.

He thought so hard that he suddenly felt them begin to grow!

They grew and grew. It happened so fast he had to get up and take off his pajama top, so they wouldn't get bent. He could hardly believe it was true.

When he tried to flex his wings, he suddenly rose off the floor and bumped his head on the ceiling. So he opened the window and flew right out!

He flew effortlessly. The moon sat like a soccer ball in the sky, and the stars glowed like cats' eyes in the dark.

Way, way down below, he saw his own street. It was no longer than his smallest stick!

And outside his house lay his tin cans shining in the moonlight.
Everyone was asleep. Nobody saw Shorty gliding like an eagle in the sky.
But pretty soon he was freezing and his teeth were chattering, since
he was wearing only his pajama bottoms. So he flew home again,
snuggled under the covers, and went straight to sleep.

The next morning there was a great commotion.

His dad hadn't come home from the office party yet, but his mom almost fainted when she saw the wings.

"For heaven's sake! It's impossible. How did you get *those*?"

"Because I wanted them, of course," said Shorty. "If you want something bad enough, you get it. You said so yourself."

"Yes, but wings ... That's so peculiar," said his mom.

"What are we going to do?"

"Fly, of course," said Shorty.

His mom didn't seem anywhere near as happy as she should be.

"Now I'll have to make alterations in all your clothes," she said, complaining. "Or else you'll set a new record for the world's worst cold. First we have to cut holes in your sweaters …"

And she rushed to get her scissors and cut holes in Shorty's sweaters before she hurried off to work.

"Remember, don't fly away before Aunt Peterson comes to look after you!" she called out, just before she disappeared into the exhaust fumes.

There was no time to lose!
Just as Aunt Peterson stepped through the door, Shorty flew out the window.

His wings worked just fine. Of course, there was quite a draft through the holes in his sweater, but it didn't matter.

Down below, in the center of the city, women were rushing in and out of department stores, with big shopping bags. And the traffic police were sneaking around the parking lots, ticketing cars.

And the cars! He saw Volvo vans practically piled one on top of the other ... The whole world lay at his feet.

Feet? Oops! When he happened to wriggle one foot, his sneaker fell off and landed right on the head of an old man.

The old man screamed as loud as he could, but when he saw who had dropped the sneaker, he screamed even louder.

"Look at that maniac! He's flying!"

Then all the ladies dropped their shopping bags, and the traffic police dropped their parking tickets, and all the men jumped into their cars and called the local TV-station on their car phones.

"Hello. There's a boy flying around. That's what I said. Hurry up, before he flies away!"

Then they jumped out of their cars again, but by that time Shorty had already flown away.

Jumbo jets thundered above him. But he didn't fly too close, because they could chop him into little pieces. The woods spread out below him. The animals tried to hide under the trees, but Shorty saw them anyway. The elks' horns stuck up between the branches, and the rabbits' eyes glowed like pearls in the moss. And he saw lots of lost dogs and a whole lot of parakeets that had flown away from home. But he didn't see his own cat. So he flew above the treetops and called out, *"Kitty! Kitty! Where are you?"*

For several hours he flew back and forth, calling, and then, just as he was beginning to get cramps in his wings, he heard a faint little "Meow." He looked down and saw two ears sticking up out of a tree.

It was his very own cat!

The cat was sniffling and crying. It had been sitting in the tree for days, and it didn't dare climb down. And no wonder! There, under the tree, sat a big dog with a soccer ball in its mouth. It was Shorty's soccer ball.

Shorty made a power dive toward the ground, grabbed his soccer ball, and, before the dog had time to blink, soared high up into the air again.

With his cat in one hand and his soccer ball in the other, Shorty glided home in the dusk.

He found his way almost at once. He recognized the street that was as short as a stick, and the tin cans shining outside his house.

He flew in through the window. His mom had come home from work, and his dad was back from the office party. They were sitting in the kitchen with Aunt Peterson, and they were all crying.

When Shorty touched down with his cat and his soccer ball, they were overjoyed. They hugged him so tight that his wings got all wrinkled!

The cat threw itself at the herring, and Shorty attacked the refrigerator, which was full of Coca-Cola and french fries.

And when they had feasted, they closed their eyes and their wings and slept like logs.

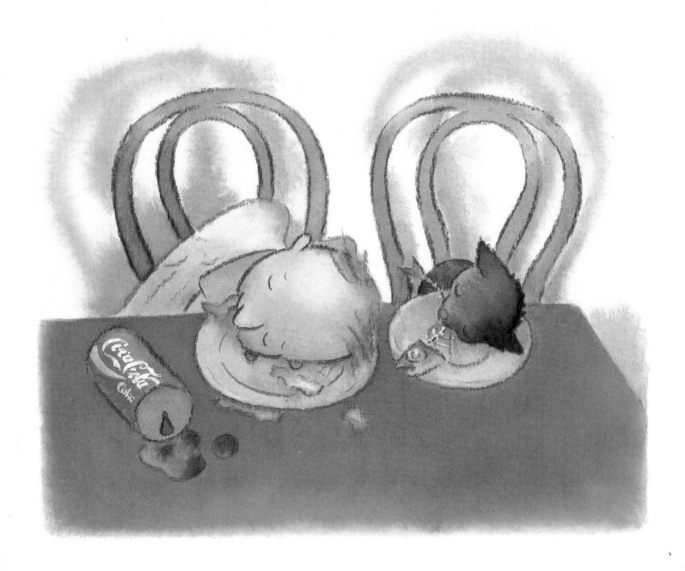

So everything came out all right in the end.

His mom altered his clothes.

The local TV-station did a program about him.

And the newspapers wrote about him until everyone was tired of hearing about his wings and didn't think they were very strange any longer.

But later, when he got bigger, his wings suddenly shrank one night and disappeared.

By that time, he was as tall as three sticks, and he no longer got lost when he walked around the block.

And the soccer ball was kicked flat.

And the cat had died.*

And later he bought himself a Volvo van!

And even later he became a rock singer!

* But it lived to be very old first and had a life full of adventure!